Exposed!

DAViD MORTiMORE BAXTER

by Karen Tayleur

illustrated by Brann Garvey

STONE ARCH BOOKS
www.stonearchbooks.com

David Mortimore Baxter is published by Stone Arch Books
151 Good Counsel Drive, P.O. Box 669
Mankato, Minnesota 56002
www.stonearchbooks.com

Library of Congress Cataloging-in-Publication Data
Tayleur, Karen.
    Exposed: In the Spotlight with David Mortimore Baxter / by Karen Tayleur;
illustrated by Brann Garvey.
    p. cm. — (David Mortimore Baxter)
    ISBN 978-1-4342-1197-2 (library binding)
    [1. Schools—Fiction. 2. Journalism—Fiction. 3. Interpersonal relations—
Fiction.] I. Garvey, Brann, ill. II. Title.
PZ7.T21149Ex 2009
[Fic]—dc22   2008031682

Summary:
David's class is in charge of producing the school's online newsletter. At first, it's
great—David loves working on the games page, Joe is a natural for DVD reviews,
and Bec is having a great time reporting. But when someone starts printing
anonymous gossip, the fun stops. Things get even worse when David suspects that
Ashley, the new girl he really likes, might be behind the vicious rumors! Can he
figure out who's spreading the gossip before things get out of hand?

Creative Director: Heather Kindseth
Graphic Designer: Carla Zetina-Yglesias

Photo Credits
Delaney Photography, cover

1 2 3 4 5 6 14 13 12 11 10 09

Printed in the United States of America

CHAPTER 1

DWAYNE KOOPERMAN

My sister, Zoe, had a boyfriend. They were officially going out. That meant that they spent a lot of time texting each other and instant messaging on the computer and talking on the phone. He even came over to our house. He came over so much that I wanted to say to him, "Do you have your own home?" I didn't, because

a) Zoe would kill me, and

b) he was way *BIGGER* than me.

It all started about two months ago. We were having dinner when **Harry** just happened to mention that some guy named Dwayne had called. Anyway, as soon as Harry mentioned Dwayne's name, Zoe sank down in her chair.

"Who's Dwayne?" I asked.

"Could you pass the salt, please, Mom?" asked Zoe, **ignoring** me.

Mom passed the salt.

"Who's Dwayne?" I repeated.

"Could you pass the bread, please, Dad?" asked Zoe, ignoring me again.

That's when I knew it was serious. Usually Zoe would YELL at me and tell me to mind my own business. She never just ignored me.

"Who's Dwayne?" I asked for a third time.

"Yes, who is Dwayne?" asked Mom. "Didn't he call yesterday, too?"

"He's just a guy," said Zoe, buttering her bread.

"A guy from school?" asked Harry.

Zoe shook her head.

"So if you didn't meet him at school, where did you meet him?" I asked.

"He's just a guy, okay?" snapped **Zoe**.

"That's enough, David," said Mom.

"What? I was just being interested in my sister's life," I said. I tried to make my face look like I really cared.

"Is he your **boyfriend**?" asked Harry.

Zoe slammed her bread down on the table. Then she said, "Yes. Okay? **YES**, he is my boyfriend. Can I be excused from the table, please?"

"No, you are still eating dinner," said Mom firmly. "Boys, please let Zoe have her **privacy**."

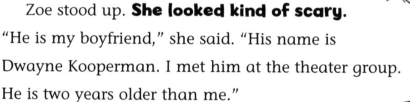

"So where did you meet this boy?" asked **Dad**.

Zoe stood up. **She looked kind of scary.** "He is my boyfriend," she said. "His name is Dwayne Kooperman. I met him at the theater group. He is two years older than me."

"Sit down, please, Zoe," said Mom. "David, could you please fill up the water jug?"

And that was the **END** of that discussion. At least for then.

* * *

I mentioned Dwayne Kooperman at the **Secret Club** meeting the next day. The Secret Club has three members: me, Joe, and Bec.

"I am **NEVER** going to get a girlfriend," I said.

"You **will** get a girlfriend," said **Bec**, smiling wisely.

"Nope," I said.

"Yep," she said.

"Never," I said.

Bec just kept nodding like she knew something I didn't.

"Bec, you think you know everything about me, but you don't," I said. "I am never going to have a girlfriend. **I just don't see the point.**"

"No girlfriends ever," Joe agreed.

But Bec just kept nodding.

* * *

The next time **Dwayne** called our home phone, Mom answered it. She invited him to lunch the next Sunday. After that, he pretty much never left. The bad thing about having Dwayne around was that he always took **the last drink of juice** in the fridge. He was always sitting in my seat when we watched TV. And he always told my mom what a good cook she was, even when she cooked her **veggie loaf**.

Sometimes, I have to admit, he was GOOD to have around. He helped me a few times with my math homework. He played one-on-one when I felt like shooting some hoops. And he was a **computer genius**. Half the time I had no idea what he was talking about, but he could fix my computer in five minutes.

And he made my sister HAPPY. That was a good thing, because when my sister is happy she isn't stomping around the house and acting like a **black hole of misery**.

So that's the story of Dwayne. Life went on pretty much like **normal**, until one day Dwayne stopped coming around.

Zoe started stomping around the house. When she wasn't stomping, she was in her room.

When I asked Mom what the problem was, she said that **Dwayne and Zoe had broken up**. They weren't girlfriend and boyfriend anymore.

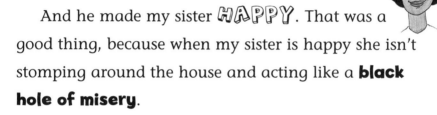

At the next Secret Club meeting, I told Bec and Joe what had happened.

"It's officially **over**," I said. "They aren't girlfriend and boyfriend anymore."

"Well, that's sad," said Bec.

"And now Zoe's miserable. She's walking around like she might bite your head off if you even look at her. Which is another reason why I'll never ever have a girlfriend," I said. **"Having a girlfriend makes you go crazy."**

"But that's love for you," said Bec. **"It's the highs. The lows. The ups. The downs."**

"Sounds like a ROLLERCOASTER to me," said Joe.

"It's Romeo and Juliet!" said Bec.

"Didn't Romeo die?" I asked.

"Actually, they both died," said Joe.

Bec ignored us. She said, "It's Cupid firing his **arrow of love** into your heart!"

"What's a cupid?" said Joe.

"Who, you mean," said Bec. "Cupid is the ancient Roman god of love."

"Well, if true love means getting shot by an **arrow**, I can do without it," I said.

Joe raised his hand. We slapped a high five. "You're right," he agreed.

And that was the end of that.

That night, Dwayne and Zoe got back together.

* * *

The next day, we had just gotten to school. Then **Ms. Stacey** asked us to be quiet. I looked up. A girl with blond hair and **the bluest eyes I'd ever seen** in my life was standing next to Ms. Stacey.

"Quiet, please, class," said Ms. Stacey. "I would like to welcome **Ashley Benton** to our class. Ashley will be with us for the rest of the year. Bec Trigg, I am hoping you can take Ashley **under your wing**. Show her around the school, that kind of thing."

Bec nodded. She moved her books so that Ashley could sit next to her.

"Okay, class," said Ms. Stacey. "Today we will be looking at . . ."

I sat still, watching Ms. Stacey's lips move, but there were two words that were crashing around inside my head — **Ashley Benton**.

My heart was doing a weird 𝕋ℍ𝕌𝕄ℙ  𝕋ℍ𝕌𝕄ℙ thing like I'd just run a marathon. I thought maybe I was having a **heart attack** or something. I must have looked strange, because Joe leaned over and asked me if I was okay.

I just nodded. But I knew I wasn't.

I had been hit in the heart by one of Cupid's stupid arrows.

CHAPTER 2

BAYS PARK IN THE SPOTLIGHT

Our school has a weekly newsletter. I used to put it in my backpack every Tuesday, and at the end of the year, I'd throw out all of the newsletters. Of course, they were handy to have in there for when I left something like a **banana** in the bottom of my bag. The newsletters helped **soak up all the mush**.

Anyway, the newsletter was put together by a bunch of parents who had **nothing better** to do with their time. You'd see them every Tuesday morning making copies and stapling papers together.

Then our school board had a **great idea**. They decided that we should publish the newsletter online to save **money** and **trees**. They thought it was a great way to make sure everyone got to read it.

Not that anyone ever read it anyway. As far as I knew.

I guess parents would probably find it helpful to find out stuff that was going on at school. (Not that I wanted Mom to know when parent-teacher conferences were.) And kids like **Rose Thornton** who were always winning awards liked to see **their names** in things like that.

Then Principal Woods had his own great idea. He decided that the students should be **in charge** of the newsletter. Ms. Stacey told us about it the day after **Ashley Benton** arrived. Everyone had something to say about it.

"I want to be the *editor*," said Rose. "I should be. I am very good at spelling. And I have a photo they can use for my weekly column."

"I could write about **monkeys**," said Jake Davern.

"We could have a **trading card section**," said Tom Chui.

Elly Van Veen suggested a **book review** section. Blake Webb said he would be happy to write a **sports column**.

"And I want to be the *editor*," said Rose for the fourth time.

"We'll see," said **Ms. Stacey**. "Each class is going to take turns producing the newsletter. We have been chosen as the LUCKY first  class, so we need to put our thinking caps on fast."

Then Ms. Stacey split us up into groups so we could discuss the newsletter. Bec and Ashley came over to sit by me and Joe.

"This could be **really cool**," said Joe. "I could write reviews on the latest DVD releases."

"Good idea," said Bec, writing the suggestion down.

I was trying not to look at Ashley, because doing that made my heart do the THUMP THUMP thing again.

"What do you think, Ashley?" asked Joe.

"Photos," said Ashley. Her voice was soft and low, so I had to lean in closer to hear. **She smelled like some kind of flower.** "I love taking photos."

Bec nodded. "We could use one whole page for photos," she said. "The school has a digital camera."

"Photos," Joe echoed, nodding.

I'd been trying to come up with an amazing idea. But all I could think was that **Ashley smelled like a flower** and if I moved a little bit closer our clothes would be touching.

"David?" asked Bec.

"**JOKES**," I blurted out.

"Jokes?" repeated Bec.

It did sound a little **lame**.

"Not just jokes," I said quickly. "A games page. A whole page full of jokes and comics and contests — that kind of thing."

"That's a great idea," said Ashley in her quiet voice.

I felt my ears turn red. My heart was beating so hard that it sounded like a construction site.

"You could draw the cartoons, Bec," said **Joe**.

"Hmm," said **Bec**. "I thought I could be a reporter. You know, go around the school and report on what's happening. The **interesting** stuff that they don't usually put in the newsletter."

"Like Victor Sneddon's lizard story?" asked Joe.

Bec nodded.

"What's Victor Sneddon's lizard story?" Ashley asked. So Bec told her.

We'd been sitting in an assembly, listening to Principal Woods talk on and on about something, when someone started shouting at the back of the hall. **Someone was in pain.**

It turned out that **Victor Sneddon**, cousin of Rose and school bully, had sneaked his **pet lizard** into assembly. For some reason, during Principal Woods's speech, the lizard had latched onto Victor's finger and **wouldn't let go**.

"That's awful," said Ashley.

"They could only get it off by putting Victor's hand under running water," said Joe.

"*Awful*," Ashley repeated.

I didn't say anything. I couldn't. Every time I tried to open my mouth, I **forgot** what I was going to say. Or my voice would 𝕊ℚ𝕌𝔼𝔸𝕂, so I'd pretend to be coughing instead.

By the end of the day, we had some really good ideas for the newsletter. Ms. Stacey made **Luke Firth** the editor. That was going to be trouble with a capital R, until Rose was put in charge of the "Bays Park in the Spotlight" page.

"So, basically I'm the *assistant editor*," explained **Rose** to anyone who would listen.

I was in charge of the fun and games page. Joe was going to write DVD reviews, but he had to show them to Ms. Stacey before they were published. Bec was going to write articles for the **Bays Park in the Spotlight** page. Ashley was happy to be official photographer.

I already had a joke for my fun and games page. I tried it out on Joe.

"Knock, knock," I said.

"Who's there?" asked **Joe**.

"Ida," I said.

"Ida who?"

"I dunno," I said.

"So, who is it?" asked Joe.

"That's the joke. Ida. I dunno," I explained.
Sometimes I wondered why I bothered.

"Okay," said Joe. **I could tell he didn't get it.**

Just then, Ashley walked over with the digital
camera. "Smile," she said.

Joe smiled. I kind of stretched my lips over
my teeth in a fake smile.

"My first official photo," said Ashley. "Thanks,
guys."

"Hey, no problem," I squeaked.

Joe left to ask Ms. Stacey a question.

"So, will you be my boyfriend?" Ashley asked me.

"Sure," I squeaked.

"Cool," she said.

And that's how I got a girlfriend.

CHAPTER 3

WRESTLING FAKES REVEALED!

The next day at lunch, Bec, Ashley, Joe, and I were sitting under the oak tree. We were talking about what we had to do for the newsletter. Bec's first assignment was to interview **Smashing Smorgan** from Wicked Wrestling Mania. Smorgan was kind of a friend of mine.

"But what does Smorgan have to do with our school newsletter?" I asked Bec.

Bec rolled her eyes. She said, "Rose called a meeting for everyone who's working on the Bays Park in the Spotlight page. She said that she didn't want just BORING school articles. She wants something that people are going to want to read."

"Like *Stars Weekly*?" asked Joe.

Bec nodded. "So, can you set up a **meeting** with Smorgan, David?" she asked.

I caught Ashley's surprised look out of the corner of my eye. You could tell she was really **impressed**.

"Sure," I said. "No problem."

"I'd L🔴VE to meet Smashing Smorgan," said Ashley.

"Let's all go to the meeting," said **Joe**.

"Okay," I said. Then I stood up. Lunch was almost over.

"Could you *help me up*, please, David?" asked Ashley.

"Um, sure," I said.

I felt the other two watching me. I held out my hand to Ashley and pulled her onto her feet.

Ashley leaned on me as she took a rock out of her shoe. Just then, **Rose Thornton** and her friends walked past and oohed.

"Ashley and David sitting in a tree," sang Rose.

"K-I-S-S-I-N-G," chanted her friends.

"Grow up, Rose," shouted Bec.

But Ashley looked **happy.**

* * *

I called Smorgan that night to set up an
interview time.

"Hello, Davey Baxter," he said. "Keeping out of
trouble?" Actually, he YELLED it into the phone.
There was lots of noise in the background.

I explained about the interview. At one point,
Smorgan said, "Hang on. I'm just putting the phone
down for a second."

There was a lot of **thumping** and **groaning**.
I heard a loud roar, like the crowd at a football
game. The next thing I heard was a ding ding ding of
a bell. Then Smorgan came back to the phone.

"Sorry about that," he said, a little out of breath.
"We're doing a special taping today for the show."

"So, about that interview," I said.

"Sure," Smorgan said. "I'd love to do it."

We set up a time for Friday after school. Smorgan
said we should come to the set of World Wrestling
Mania.

When **Ms. Stacey** found out we were going, she **insisted** on driving us there.

"A member of the teaching staff should be present," she explained.

In fact, Ms. Stacey had a 𝒞ℛ𝒰𝒮ℋ on Smashing Smorgan. That was the **real reason** she wanted to take us.

When we got to the WWM studio, we had to wait for Smorgan to come out of his dressing room. A couple of other wrestlers came out and said hi to us. Dr. Sleep, who looked **much shorter** than he did on TV, gave Joe his autograph. Harvey Hangman and Kenzan Kyoto got into the ring and posed for some pictures.

"Show us an **Anaconda Vice**," said Ashley as she took pictures. "That's great. Now a **Hammerlock**. Mr. Hangman, could you move your head up a little so I can see your face? 𝔽𝔸ℕ𝕋𝔸𝕊𝕋𝕀ℂ."

"How does she know so much about wrestling?" whispered Joe.

"I guess she did her homework," I said, smiling.

"Which is more than you ever do," Bec added.

Harvey and Kenzan posed a few more times. Then Harvey climbed the ropes and jumped down on Kenzan's back. Kenzan fell to the mat.

"Ohhhh," said Bec. "Is he all right?"

Kenzan looked up and winked. *"All in a day's work,"* he said.

Then Smorgan came out and talked to Bec and Joe. Ms. Stacey stayed in the background. Her eyelashes were batting so much that I thought **there was something stuck in her eye.**

"Are you okay?" I asked.

"Of course, David," she said with a giggle, her eyelashes batting faster.

After Bec was done interviewing Smorgan, I introduced **Ashley** to him.

"Could I take a picture of you, please, Mr. Smorgan?" asked Ashley.

"And who's this young lady?" asked Smorgan. "Is she your 𝒢𝐼ℛℒ𝐹ℛ𝐼𝐸𝒩𝒟, Davey?"

"Yeah right," said Bec with a snort.

Ashley just giggled. **I nodded.**

"What?" said Joe.

Then **Bec** didn't say anything. I guess it's pretty hard to talk when your jaw is scraping the ground.

When I got home, I put together my fun and games page for the newsletter. It was due the next day. Joe had written his DVD review, but he wanted to polish it up and find a picture to go with it. Bec had to write her Smorgan article, so she didn't have time to hang out. I know she was dying to find out what the story was with Ashley and me.

I guess I was too.

I emailed my fun and games page to Luke so he could edit it over the weekend. Ms. Stacey said he could also have extra time on Monday after school, but it **definitely** had to be finished by 5 p.m.

Over the weekend, Bec and Joe came over and we hung out. Mostly, we practiced SPYING on my neighbor, Mr. McCafferty. I could tell they wanted to ask about Ashley, but they didn't.

Anyway, I really didn't know what to say. She said she was my girlfriend, but nothing else had changed.

I was **kind of excited** to see my fun and games page on the Internet on Tuesday. Oh, and the rest of the newsletter, too, I guess. Principal Woods made a big deal about launching the newsletter.  He got on a webcam and was beamed into every classroom with a computer. Students were allowed to spend fifteen minutes of school time reading the newsletter online.

When it was my turn, I went straight to the fun and games page. **It looked great.** Luke had made it look good, but it was the quality of the jokes that really stood out.

Joe's DVD review was good, too.

Then I went to the **Bays Park in the Spotlight** page to read the Smashing Smorgan interview by Bec.

A great photo by Ashley was splashed across the top of the screen. The picture showed Harvey Hangman perched on the back of Kenzan Kyoto, who was looking up at the camera and winking. The headline read **"Wrestling Fakes Revealed!"**

"No!" I mumbled.

At the bottom of the page there was a little article with the headline "Bays Park Shorts." There were messages about lost books, an invitation to join the school chess club, and a list of what was for lunch that week. Right down at the bottom, there was a small paragraph with the headline **"Bays Park Shines the Light."**

Which well-known Bays Park teacher was seen hanging around the stage door of TV idol Smashing Smorgan last Friday? Could there be wedding bells in the air? Stay tuned to this spotlight for further updates.

"Oh no," I moaned. "Bec, what have you done?"

CHAPTER 4

PURPLE, PINK, OR BLUE?

There was a big reaction to the first Bays Park Newsletter Online. **Not all of it was good.**

First of all, there were a few people who didn't agree with Joe's DVD review. And they let him know it. I had forgotten to send answers for my game page, so **Luke** was **mad at me** about that.

But the thing that most people were talking about was the **World Wrestling Mania** story.

When Bec saw me coming over to talk to her, she held up her hand. "Whoa. Stop right there," she said. "I'm over it. I don't want to talk about it anymore." She told me that she'd already heard from a lot of loyal WWM fans. **That included Ms. Stacey.**

"But how could you?" I asked. "You made Smashing Smorgan and his friends look like a bunch of *fakers*. And you basically told everyone that Ms. Stacey and Smashing Smorgan were getting married."

"I did not write that GOSSIP about Ms. Stacey and Smashing Smorgan. And yes, I did write the article about World Wrestling Mania but I didn't write that headline. The headline had nothing to do with what I wrote," said Bec. "And maybe **your girlfriend** needs to be more careful when she takes pictures. You know what they say — **a picture is worth a thousand words.**"

"Well, it's not Ashley's fault," I said.

"Oh, really?" said Bec. "So **it's my fault**? Nice to know who your friends are." Then she walked away before I could say anything else.

That morning, **Ms. Stacey** talked to us about our first newsletter. "What a wonderful job you have done so far," she said. "There were only a few small problems." When she said that, she looked right at Bec.

"Anyway," Ms. Stacey continued, "I hope you are already thinking about next week's newsletter. I would like to have a meeting with the editor at lunch today."

Luke Firth nodded. He frowned and tried to look **important.**

"Blake, there's a baseball game against St. Jude's this Friday," Ms. Stacey said. "That would make a **great article.** And don't forget to get lots of photos. There really were some EXCELLENT pictures in this week's newsletter."

I looked at **Ashley**, whose cheeks creased into a **dimple.** Next to her, Bec scowled.

Rose Thornton put her hand in the air. She waved it around like she was **drying nail polish** or something.

"Yes, Rose?" said Ms. Stacey.

"I would like to call a BPITS meeting for this lunchtime," said Rose.

She was wearing glasses, although I know for a fact that she doesn't need to wear glasses to see. She also had a pen stuck above her ear just in case she quickly had to write an AMAZING fact down.

"BPITS?" asked Ms. Stacey.

"Bays Park in the Spotlight," explained Rose.

A couple of people **groaned**.

Ms. Stacey nodded. "Okay, Rose," she said. "You can use our classroom for a meeting space."

We had three weeks left before the newsletter moved to another class. My next fun and games page was going to be 𝔽𝔸ℕ𝕋𝔸𝕊𝕋𝕀ℂ. I started planning for it right away. Unfortunately, we were supposed to be working on Chapter 3 in our math book.

"Is that math, David Baxter?" Ms. Stacey asked.

She'd caught me red-handed. Really. **My red pen had leaked everywhere.**

I shook my head. "It's the fun and games page," I explained.

"Put it away, please," she said.

* * *

Since we'd started working on the newsletter, Joe, Bec, and I never hung out at lunchtime anymore. Joe kept going to the library to research directors or producers or other things about movies.

By Thursday at lunch, I hadn't talked to Bec since Tuesday except to say **"Hi"** or **"Bye."** She was too busy working on her articles for the newsletter.

So lunch always ended up just being me and Ashley. That was kind of 𝔸𝕎𝕂𝕎𝔸ℝ𝔻. I mean, I had no idea what to say to her. Luckily she did all the talking.

"What do you think about purple, David?" she asked me.

"It's okay," I said. **What else could I say?**

"But I mean, do you think it's better than pink? Or would you prefer blue?" Ashley asked.

I said, "I think purple is fine."

"Oh," she said. You could tell she was disappointed in my answer because her dimples disappeared.

"But **pink is good** too," I added. "And blue. Blue is good."

I wasn't sure what the right answer was. **I wasn't even sure what the question was.**

"Do you like cats or dogs?" Ashley asked me.

"Umm, both," I said.

"You have to choose one," she said with a pout. Then she kind of shoved me lightly. That made my heart THUMP a little louder.

"Dogs," I said.

"Oh," she said. She pouted again.

Obviously, dogs was the wrong answer.

"But cats are cool too," I said.

Being alone with Ashley just made me feel CONFUSED. I didn't understand what I was supposed to do. I thought maybe I should give her a **present**, but I was too scared I'd pick the wrong type of present.

"Bec has a pet rat named Ralph," I added.

"Oooh," Ashley said, wrinkling her nose. "*Rats are so dirty.*"

"Actually, Ralph is really clean," I explained. "He even does **tricks**."

"I hate rats," said Ashley. "*Hate.*"

"So, do you have a cat?" I asked.

Ashley didn't have a cat. She had a cat once, but it had died from old age. It had been about **96 years old** in cat years.

A few days ago, Ashley had seen a kitten in the local pet store. She told me all about the kitten.

It was white and fluffy. It had a little pink nose. It looked like it was wearing **three black socks**.

I tried changing the subject a few times, but all Ashley wanted to talk about was the kitten. Somewhere in all that kitten talk she managed to mention that her **birthday** was coming up very soon.

My heart began to $\mathbb{THUMP}$ loudly again. Her birthday. **The pressure was on.** Was I supposed to buy Ashley a present? Of course I was. But how much money was I supposed to spend? Should I ask what she wanted, or was I just supposed to know?

Finally, the bell rang. Ashley and I were walking back to class. Then I saw **Victor Sneddon**. He was frowning at me. I must have looked how I felt. **And I felt terrible.**

For a split second, I thought about asking Victor Sneddon for **advice about girls**. But then he pushed me out of the way and the moment passed.

CHAPTER 5

TOYS 4 US

That night I asked Zoe about buying Ashley a present. I knew if I told her **the truth** I would never hear the end of it. So I made up a story.

"Zoe, can I ask you a question?" I asked. I was standing in her doorway because she hadn't said I could come in.

"Is this important?" asked Zoe. She was tapping away at her keyboard.

"Yep," I said.

"Then come in and shut the door," said **Zoe**.
"Don't touch anything."

I waited for her to finish closing down all her instant messaging screens. I noticed the last person she said goodbye to was **Dwayne**. I could tell it was him, because there was a picture of them together in the top of his screen.

GROSS!

"So. What?" Zoe asked.

"A friend of mine has a problem," I began.

"A friend?" repeated Zoe.

I nodded. "This friend of mine has a girlfriend," I explained. **"He's never had a girlfriend before."**

"Your friend," said Zoe.

I nodded again. Then I said, "Anyway, his girlfriend is having a birthday. **And he doesn't know what to buy her.** I mean, he doesn't have a lot of money anyway, but he has to buy her something. So how much should he spend? Should he ask her what she wants?"

"What kinds of things does this girl like?" asked Zoe.

"She likes kittens," I said. "And I think she likes purple better than pink, but I'm not really sure about that. I do know she doesn't like blue. And she hates rats. **She definitely hates rats."**

"How old is she?" asked Zoe.

"About my age," I said.

Zoe said, "Kittens cost a lot of money. Besides, **you can't give a kitten to someone as a present**. Her parents might not want a cat. But you could buy her a stuffed animal. A stuffed kitten that she could keep on her bed."

"You mean **my friend** could buy her that," I corrected.

Zoe smiled and nodded. Then her cell phone beeped. She picked it up, read her message, then started texting.

"Okay, well, thanks," I said, as I left her bedroom.

"Do you need any money for that present?" asked Zoe.

"I have enough for a toy kitten," I said.

It wasn't until later that I realized I'd blown my cover.

＊ ＊ ＊

The next day, I asked **Bec** if she would come shopping with me.

"Shopping?" said Bec. "For what?"

"Ashley's birthday is coming up," I explained. "I need to buy her a present."

Bec seemed ANNOYED, but she agreed to go to the mall with me after school that day. I asked **Joe** to come along, but he said he was **too busy**. He had to go home and watch some DVDs for his newsletter column.

Bec and I went to the mall after school. We only had an hour before we had to be home.

First, we headed for Toys 4 Us. **The store was huge**. We spent the first half hour walking around, just looking at the stuff on the shelves.

"Wow, look at this airbrush," said Bec, pulling a box off the shelf. "It even comes with paint."

"We're running out of time," I said, grabbing Bec by the arm.

Bec shoved the box back onto the shelf.

"So, what do you want to buy?" she asked angrily.

"A toy kitten," I said.

Finally, twenty minutes later, we found the stuffed animals. Bec picked up a black cat with green eyes.

"How about this one?" she asked.

I shook my head. "It has to be white and **fluffy**," I said.

Then Bec picked up a white and fluffy cat with blue eyes. "What about this?" she asked.

I shook my head again. "It has to be a kitten," I said. "A white fluffy kitten with a pink nose and black socks."

The stuffed animals were in a large wire basket. I could see some **white fluff** at the bottom of the basket, so I started pulling the toys out onto the floor.

Suddenly, from out of nowhere, a Toys 4 Us salesperson appeared. **"Aren't you a little old for stuffed animals?"** he asked.

"It's not for me," I said. I kept leaning over into the basket. I was only halfway down.

"Of course not," said the salesperson. "I suppose it's for your friend." I saw him look at Bec.

"It's not for me," said Bec. "I'd rather have an airbrush. It's for his girlfriend."

"Oh," said the salesperson.

I finally reached the white fluffy toy. But it was a **white fluffy gorilla**. I groaned.

"What are you looking for?" asked the salesperson. "Perhaps I can help?"

There was no fluffy white kitten with black socks and a pink nose in the entire store. I ended up buying a fluffy white kitten with a pink nose and no socks. Bec had to lend me some **extra cash** to pay for it.

"I hope she's worth it," Bec said.

I wasn't sure what to say, so I just nodded.

Bec didn't talk to me all the way home. And we ended up being late, too.

GRAPES AND ALIENS

On Saturday, Joe, Bec, and I were sitting around in my kitchen. We were waiting for Mom's **newest creation** to come out of the oven. Bec still didn't have her story written for BPITS. She wasn't sure what to write about.

"You could interview a movie star," suggested Joe.

Bec rolled her eyes. "How many **movie stars** do you know, Joe?" she asked.

Joe shrugged. "Rose Thornton knows some," he suggested.

"I'm not asking Rose," said Bec.

"You could interview the principal," I said.

"𝕭𝕺𝕽𝕴𝕹𝕲," said Joe.

"I want to write a good news story," said Bec. "I just don't know any good news."

"Why don't we go to the mall?" I said. "You could **interview** people. Someone will have a good news story."

"That's a good idea!" said Bec, smiling.

"Great. **I'll call Ashley.** She'll bring her camera to take pictures," I said.

Bec stopped smiling. "Great," she said. "Can't wait."

I had the feeling that Bec didn't like Ashley, but I wasn't sure why. What wasn't to like about her? She was **perfect**! She had **cute dimples** and a **flower smell**!

I called Ashley and told her to meet us at the mall.

"Hey, great," she said. "We can go on a *double date.*"

When she hung up, I felt **WEIRD**. The idea of going on a date was bad enough, but the idea of Joe and Bec being on a date together was just **wrong**. I decided not to tell them what Ashley had said. I hoped that she wouldn't mention it when we met up at the mall.

* * *

At the mall, we went to the information desk. Bec asked if we could interview some people for the school newsletter.

"I don't see why not," said the man behind the desk. "You can stand to the side here and **I'll keep an eye on you.**"

Whenever someone came to the information desk, Bec tried to interview them. Most people were too busy. I kept looking for Ashley, but **she was late.**

After about ten minutes, Rose Thornton walked past with her friends. They were all dressed up like they were **going to the Oscars** or something. They were wearing high heels and makeup and stuff.

Rose didn't even bother to **stop and talk**. She just sort of waved at us, which was fine with me.

"Where is Ashley?" Bec kept asking. "I need pictures for my story."

Finally, Ashley walked up. "Hey guys," she shouted.

"She looks like a grape," mumbled Bec.

Ashley did kind of look like a grape. She was wearing **purple** everything, right down to her shoes. Luckily, I like grapes.

When she walked up, Ashley gave Bec a huge hug. **Bec's eyes almost popped out of her head.**

"Um, hello," mumbled Bec.

"How are you, Joe?" asked Ashley. She grabbed his arm in a friendly way.

Joe turned red. He nodded and said, "Good."

Then Ashley shoved the camera into his hand. She turned to me and took my hand. "David, you *must* come with me," she said, pulling me away. "I have to show you something. Be right back," she shouted over her shoulder to the others.

Ashley dragged me to a shop called **Pet Parade**, which is where my brother, Harry, always wants to go when we come to the mall. **I like animals**, but I am not crazy about the pet store.

"Look," said Ashley. She pointed to a very white and very fluffy kitten. "Isn't she the CUTEST?"

We spent at least half an hour looking at the kitten and her playmates. Then we spent another half hour stopping and looking in store windows while Ashley pointed out things that I really wasn't interested in. **Shopping is my least favorite thing to do**, besides homework.

Finally, an hour later, we got back to the information desk. I felt GUILTY about being away so long.

Bec was in the middle of writing down some notes while **a man with a bald head and very big ears** talked quietly to her.

Joe handed Ashley's camera back to her. "That guy doesn't want his photo taken," he said. "I think Bec wants to get rid of him. He says he's been abducted by aliens twice in the last week."

Finally, the man walked away from Bec.

"Well, thank you very much for that," said Bec as the man walked away.

"Excuse me," said Ashley loudly. The man
turned around and Ashley quickly took some pictures.

"Hey!" the man yelled. **Then he scurried away.**

"How's it going, Bec?" I asked.

"Fine," she said. "Joe was really helpful. I think I
have enough to write about."

"Great," said Ashley. "Let's go get
something to eat. I'm *starving*."

In the food court, Bec talked about some of her
interviews. "There's a few that I could choose
from," she said. "There was a group of scouts
holding a fund-raiser for their new scout hall.
And I talked to a woman who was last year's Bays
Park Citizen of the Year."

"I took pictures," said **Joe**, pointing to
the camera.

Ashley looked through the pictures on the camera.
"Hey, there are some good ones in here," she
said. "Good work, Joe."

Bec picked up her notebook. She tore off the last page. "I definitely won't be using this **abducted by aliens** story," she said. She CRUMPLED  the paper up and pushed it into the middle of the table.

Then Ashley told them all about the kitten in the pet store and the things she'd seen on sale. She just kept going **on and on** about it. I could tell the others were getting BORED. I certainly was.

"No wonder you were gone for so long," grumbled Bec.

But Ashley **ignored** her and just kept talking.

Later, I couldn't remember if the piece of story with Bec's alien story had still been on the table when we left. Of course, by the time it mattered, **there was nothing I could do about it anyway.**

CHAPTER 7

ALIEN ABDUCTION HORROR

On Tuesday, when the newsletter came out, everyone wanted to see the BPITS page right away. The headline said, **"Alien Abduction Horror!"**

Ms. Stacey stomped into the classroom ten minutes late on Tuesday morning, plonked her books on the desk, then went back to shut the door behind her. *She looked furious.*

"I have just been to Principal Woods's office," she said. Her voice sounded kind of 𝖂𝕰𝕴𝕽𝕯. My voice does that when I have to see the principal too. I just didn't think **teachers** would feel the same way.

"And I must say he is very *disappointed* with this class. Very," Ms. Stacey repeated. "The story about being **abducted by aliens** was not what I approved. I approved a **nice story** about some scouts raising money. Principal Woods is disappointed with you, and so am I."

There was total silence.

"Bec Trigg, please stand up," said Ms. Stacey.

Bec's face was already 𝗥𝗘𝗗. She stood up and opened her mouth.

Ms. Stacey held up her hand. "Just tell me this, please," said Ms. Stacey. "Did you or did you not interview this man for the alien abduction article? **Yes or no?**"

"The thing is," Bec started.

"Just yes or no, please," Ms. Stacey said.

Bec nodded and whispered, **"Yes."**

"I see," Ms. Stacey said. "Sit down please. Rose Thornton, please stand up."

Rose stood up. She was still wearing her **fake glasses**, which she pushed back up her nose as they slid forward.

"Did you edit this story for your Spotlight page?" asked Ms. Stacey.

"BPITS," corrected Rose.

"Yes or no?" yelled Ms. Stacey.

"I *really liked* the scout story," said Rose.

"So how did this story end up in the newsletter?" asked Ms. Stacey.

Rose shrugged. "Maybe you should ask the editor," she said, pointing at **Luke Firth**. I looked over at Luke. He looked 𝕄𝕀𝕊𝔼ℝ𝔸𝔹𝕃𝔼.

"Sit down please," said Ms. Stacey. "Ashley?"

Ashley stood up.

"Did you take this photo?" Ms. Stacey asked.

Ashley nodded. **Then she burst into tears.** "But I didn't think Bec was going to use that story," she explained.

"Sit down, please, Ashley," said Ms. Stacey gently. "I'm not sure what has gone on here, but **I am going to get to the bottom of it.** Luke, Bec, and Rose, I would like you to stay inside at recess to talk about this. Now, get out your notebooks. We are going to have a math test."

I had never seen Ms. Stacey so mad before.

It turned out that the man in the alien story had somehow found out about the newsletter. He was thinking about **suing the school**. That was incredibly bad luck.

Bec told Joe and me later that at the recess meeting with Ms. Stacey, there was no chance to get to the truth because Ms. Stacey was so busy being mad at them all. Bec wasn't sure how the **mix-up** had happened, especially since she'd ripped the story out of her notebook.

"Someone must have picked it up after we left the food court," said Bec. "**But who?** And why would they? Luke swears that he never even saw that story before today."

I had an idea about how the story had gotten into the newsletter, but I wasn't going to tell Bec. Not yet, anyway. First I had to talk to **Ashley**.

After school, I met her in the parking lot. She seemed quiet. There was no sign of a dimple and her eyes looked like she might have been CRYING again.

"David," she said, "thank you for waiting. It's been such a *horrible* day."

The next thing I knew I was carrying her bag. That was fine, but **I was already carrying my own backpack.**

"So, about today," I said.

"It was awful," said Ashley, shaking her head. "Really awful. *I think it was one of the worst days of my life.*"

She wasn't making it very 𝑒𝑎𝑠𝑦 for me to talk to her.

"I was thinking about how that story got into the newsletter," I began.

"I know. It's so 𝕊𝕋ℝ𝔸ℕ𝔾𝔼," said Ashley. "I mean, Bec threw that story away at the mall and somehow it ended up in the newsletter. Someone must have picked it up."

I nodded. "Someone who was working on the newsletter," I said. "I mean, how else would the story end up in the newsletter?"

Ashley frowned. "Did you hear that Rose and Luke had a **fight** about this week's newsletter?" she asked.

"That doesn't surprise me," I said. Rose Thornton was **always** fighting with someone.

"And did you hear that Mr. Bishop's car was parked outside Ms. Stacey's house last Sunday night until *really late?*" she added.

"No," I said. I didn't really care about Mr. Bishop's car. Mr. Bishop was a music teacher.

"Do you think Mr. Bishop is *Ms. Stacey's boyfriend?*" asked Ashley.

Mr. Bishop was about 100 years old, so I didn't think so. "No," I said. This conversation was making me yawn.

"Anyway," Ashley said, "my mom wants you to come to my birthday dinner on Friday night. Did I mention it was my *BIRTHDAY?*"

I nodded.

"Well, every year I get to invite a **best friend**," she said, "and this year it's you."

"Great," I said. "What do you **want** for your birthday?" I wanted to pretend I didn't have a present.

"Oh, you don't have to get me anything," she said. "*Just having you there* for dinner will be enough for me."

𝕣𝔸𝕋𝕊! I had spent over $20 on a present for Ashley and she didn't even care if I gave her a present or not. What a waste of money.

* * *

That night I talked to Bec about it.

"She didn't mean it," said **Bec**.

"What?" I asked.

"When she said she didn't want you to buy her anything, she didn't really mean it. That's just what girls say," Bec explained.

"I don't get it," I said. "Why can't girls just **say what they mean**?"

"She was being polite," said Bec. "Can we stop talking about Ashley? I really want to talk about the alien story. **I am in so much trouble!**"

I was pretty sure that I knew what had happened, but I didn't have any proof.

"**I have an idea.** I think we can find out what happened. But you and Joe are going to have to help me," I said.

"Tell me," said Bec.

"I think this is Secret Club business," I said. "**Operation Unmask.** I'm calling a meeting for lunchtime tomorrow at school."

"But what about Ashley?" asked Bec. "She's not in the Secret Club. How are we going to 𝔇𝕴𝕿𝕮𝕳 her at lunchtime."

"You leave Ashley to me," I said.

* * *

It wasn't until later, when I got to read the newsletter again, that I noticed a small notice in the Bays Park Shorts section.

"**Endless Love,**" read the headline.

I read the article. Then I read it again.

I couldn't believe it.

She'd really gone too far this time.

Which chess man's car was seen outside a favorite Bays Park teacher's house late Sunday night? Stay tuned for more details . . .

CHAPTER 8

JEALOUS?

The next morning, I met up with Ashley under the oak tree. I told her that I had to help the librarian **count books** at lunchtime.

"That's okay," she said. "I'll just hang out with Bec and Joe."

"Um, I think they're busy too," I said.

Ashley touched my hand and my heart did its THUMPING thing.

"Is there something wrong?" she asked me. "David, you'd tell me, wouldn't you?"

I tried to change the subject. "Two days until your birthday," I said.

Ashley smiled and said, "I know. I can hardly wait." Then she started talking about her birthday and I didn't get a word in until school started.

* * *

The Secret Club has a **secret place** to meet at school, but we only use it in emergencies. **And this was an emergency.**

When the lunch bell rang, I raced outside and headed straight for our spot. There's a fence covered in ivy on one side of our school. The ivy is so thick that you can sneak in, cover yourself with leaves, and **no one will ever find you.** The problem is, sometimes it takes a while to find the rest of the Secret Club members.

There are only three **Secret Club** members — Joe, Bec and me. I had been really close to asking Ashley to join, but I wasn't sure Bec would be too happy with that idea.

I thought I'd reached the secret spot first. But when I crashed through the leaves, I almost fell into **Joe's** lap. "Hey, 𝕮𝕬𝕽𝕰𝕱𝖀𝕷," he said.

We waited another five minutes for Bec to show up.

"Okay, so what's going on?" asked Joe when Bec finally arrived.

"I know how that alien story got into the school newsletter," I said.

"**Did an alien put it there?**" asked Joe.

Bec rolled her eyes. "Don't be silly," she said.

"It was Ashley," I said. The words stuck in my throat like peanut butter. **Crunchy peanut butter**, of course.

"What?" said Joe.

"No way," said Bec.

"It makes sense," I said. "Look, we were all at the mall. Bec ripped out the page and put it on the table. There was **no one else** who works on the BPITS page at that table except Bec."

"And I didn't publish it," said Bec.

"I believe you," I said, but **it made my heart do a little flip.**

"Maybe it was someone else? Maybe a stranger picked it up," said Joe.

"And then the **stranger** came to our school and published the story without Luke knowing?" I said.

- 61 -

I shook my head. Then I said, "Come on, Joe. **It was Ashley.** We all know it."

"But why would she do it?" asked **Bec**, who is usually SMARTER than all of us.

"I don't know," I said.

"She's **jealous**," said Joe, snapping his fingers.

"Jealous of who?" asked Bec.

"Jealous of you, of course," said Joe. "She's David's girlfriend and **she wants him all to herself**. I guess she doesn't like that you've known him longer. So she's trying to WRECK BPITS so that it will make you look bad."

"No," said Bec.

"Yes," said Joe, nodding his head. "It's exactly what happened in this **movie** called 'Now You See Me Now You Don't'."

I shook my head. I hated the thought that sweet, dimpled Ashley could be so mean. But I did think she had something to do with the **newsletter problem**, and Joe's story did kind of make sense.

"So now what?" asked Joe.

We all sat there wondering what to do next. The wind whistled through the leaves and let in a thin ray of light.

"Now we move on to Operation BPITS," I said. **An idea hit me.**

Then the bell rang and we had to run to get back inside in time. I knew the others were dying to know what my plan was, but I still hadn't figured it out yet. All I knew was that we had to prove that **Ashley was trying to make Bec look bad**. And we had to do it soon.

When Ashley smiled at me in the classroom as we took our seats, my heart didn't do its normal 𝒯𝓗𝓤𝓜𝓟 𝒯𝓗𝓤𝓜𝓟 thing. Instead, **the peanut butter feeling** was back in my throat when I tried to smile back.

CHAPTER 9

OPERATION BPITS

The next day I tried to **avoid** Ashley while I figured out a plan for **Operation BPITS**. At lunchtime, I said I had to talk to Ms. Stacey about an assignment that was due.

Then I sneaked outside and spied on Ashley. She was sitting under the oak tree like she was **waiting** for me.

I'd been watching her for about ten minutes when I could feel someone's **hot breath** on my neck.

"What are you doing?" a voice rumbled.

I didn't have to turn around to know who it was. "Hi, Victor," I said.

Did I mention that **Victor** was the school bully? Having Victor Sneddon **breathing down your neck** was not something you ever wished for.

"So?" he asked. "What are you doing?"

"I'm **HIDING**," I said. I figured there was no point telling him a **lie**.

"I guessed that," Victor said. "So why are you hiding from your girlfriend?"

I didn't know how to answer that one.

"She is your girlfriend, right?" he demanded.

"She was," I said.

"Oh. I get it," said Victor. Then he kind of grunted and left me alone.

The longer I let Ashley wait for me, the worse I felt. She started **chewing on her nails**, which is something she did when she was nervous. **I felt really bad**, but what she had done to Bec was worse. So I just hid there and watched until the bell rang.

When I got back to my desk, I tried not to look at her face. I could tell she was looking at me.

"Ashley's looking at you," Joe told me.

"I know," I said.

"She's still looking at you," said Joe.

It was going to be a long day.

* * *

The next day was Ashley's birthday. I still hadn't figured out the plan for Operation BPITS and I was still AVOIDING Ashley.

I didn't have to avoid her too long, though. She came right up to me as I sat down at my desk in the morning. She said, "You're not invited to my birthday dinner any more. Someone else is coming." Then she marched back to her desk.

"Well, that lets you off the hook," said Joe.

"Yeah," I said. I tried to sound like **I didn't care**, but a part of me wanted to know who was going to her birthday dinner instead of me.

I noticed that Bec gave Ashley a birthday card, which was kind of STRANGE. I asked Bec about it later. Bec explained, "It would look stranger if I didn't. She might notice that something is up."

"Well, I guess there's no reason for **Operation BPITS** anymore," I said. "She hates me since I've been avoiding her."

Bec shook her head. "You really don't know anything about GIRLS, do you David?" she said.

Joe shook his head too.

"Explain it to him, Joe," said Bec.

Joe looked worried. "I think you should  explain it," he said.

I could tell that **Joe had no idea** what was going on.

"The thing is, David," said Bec, "Ashley is just trying to make you feel **jealous**. She thinks that you dumped her. So she's **pretending** she doesn't care and that she already has another boyfriend."

"Oh," I said. I still didn't get it. "So Operation BPITS is still on?" I asked.

"I wouldn't be surprised if there's another special little news story in the BPITS this week," Bec said. "And I don't want to end up in 𝕋ℝ𝕆𝕌𝔹𝕃𝔼 again."

"So what are we going to do?" asked Joe.

"Remember how Principal Woods used a webcam to tell us about the newsletter?" said **Bec**.

Joe and I nodded.

"Well, we just need to set that up on Monday afternoon before we leave school," Bec told us. "Then we can watch **from home** to see what happens."

"You think Ashley will be caught on the webcam?" I asked.

Bec nodded. She explained, "She's going to have to use the **special computer** in the computer lab. The one that has the software for the newsletter."

"But there is no webcam on that computer," said Joe.

"We need to set one up," said Bec.

"I know **just the person** who can help us," I said.

* * *

Having a **sister** sometimes comes in handy. Especially when that sister has a boyfriend who is good with computers. Luckily, Zoe and Dwayne hadn't had a ꟻ𝐈𝐆𝐇𝐓 since Dwayne had told Zoe he didn't like her **new shirt**. (To be fair, she asked him and he just told the truth. Even I know **that wasn't very smart**.)

When I asked **Dwayne** if he could help us set up the webcam so that we could see it at home, he said sure. He brought over some old equipment  he had. Then he drew a **diagram** so we could set it up at school.

"That looks easy," said Bec.

"Easy peasy," Dwayne agreed.

Joe and I both nodded, but I had no idea what they were talking about.

It was Friday night and **somebody else** was having birthday dinner with Ashley.

It should have been me. It should have been me watching those dimples, giving her the perfect present and smelling her flower smell. Instead, I was plotting to reveal her as a traitor. But it was me who felt like the traitor.

I wished I'd never met Ashley Benton.

CHAPTER 10

TWEAKING THE TRUTH

That weekend I just **sat around**. I wanted to call Bec and Joe and tell them I wanted to stop Operation BPITS, but I couldn't think of a good reason. I didn't think that *feeling bad* was a good enough reason.

At lunch on Monday, I noticed Ashley standing in line with Victor Sneddon.

Victor Sneddon? No way. He probably just happened to be there at the same time she was.

I decided I really needed something from the lunch line. I walked over and looked at Ashley as if I'd just seen her.

"Oh, hi," I said. Actually, it was more of a SQUEAK.

"Hello," she said. She was wearing purple again. It was a new purple jacket that I hadn't seen before.

"How was your **birthday**?" I asked.

"*Good,*" she said.

"Oh," I said. "Good."

We took a step forward in line.

"New jacket?" I asked.

"What?" she asked.

"Is that a **new jacket**?" I asked.

"Yes," she said, looking at it. "I got it for my birthday."

I could see Victor giving me a look. It was **never good** if Victor Sneddon gave you a look. Seeing that look should have made me leave. Instead, I **ignored** him.

"Ashley, I think **we need to talk**," I said.

"Hey," said Victor. "Let's go, Ash."

Ashley gave me a little wave. "See ya," I said.

Then I couldn't wait for three o'clock to roll around. I couldn't wait for **Operation BPITS** to finally begin.

* * *

The bell rang at three o'clock and everyone **rushed** out of class. Bec, Joe, Luke, and I went to the computer lab to work on the newsletter. Ms. Stacey came, too, but after a while she looked **BORED**. "I think you have this **under control**," she said. Then she left.

"Okay," I whispered to Joe and Bec. "Let's do this."

Bec distracted Luke by **arguing** about how to spell a word. Joe and I set up the webcam on the newsletter computer. Dwayne had hidden the camera in a tissue box, which we placed on top of the monitor.

"Let's go," I said when we were finished.

I couldn't wait to get home and check out the webcam from my home computer. When Joe and I got to my house, Dwayne was sitting in front of the computer. He was watching the screen.

"Hey, dudes," Dwayne said. "Check it out."

We could see Luke Firth typing something into the computer at school. Bec was behind him.

"Did you tell **Bec** we were done?" I asked Joe.

"Nope. I thought you did," said Joe.

I sent Joe back to school to get Bec. Dwayne and I watched the screen. **It got boring pretty quickly.** Finally, Joe appeared behind Luke and waved at the camera.

"Get out of there, Joe," I whispered, as if he could hear me.

Luke sat there for another half an hour. After he left, nothing happened for a while. Then Rose Thornton showed up and worked on the school computer for a while. **After Rose left, nothing happened.**

Soon, Dwayne left my house. Joe and Bec showed up at my house and sat next to me. "Thanks for leaving me there," said Bec.

"What's that?" asked Joe. He pointed at the monitor. It was a janitor, walking past the screen.

Bec and Joe stayed as LATE as they could, and then Joe's mom picked them up. I couldn't go outside to say goodbye because **I was too busy** watching the computer screen.

I was still watching when **Mom** came in to tell me it was time for bed.

"Just **five more minutes**," I pleaded.

Nothing happened for those five minutes. **Maybe nothing was going to happen.** Maybe I would never find out who had been sabotaging the school newsletter. Maybe I was an idiot who had just lost his first girlfriend for the wrong reason.

Before I went to bed I put Ashley's wrapped birthday present into my backpack.

* * *

The next day, I got to school early to read the newsletter. Everything seemed normal. Bec's article on Red Balloon Day for Reading Week seemed boring enough. Joe's DVD page looked good. My fun and games page looked **better than ever**.

Bec and Joe walked into the classroom five minutes later.

"So?" asked Joe.

"Nothing," I said, shaking my head.

"Go back to **BPITS**," demanded Bec.

We scrolled down the page. Everything looked *normal*.

"What about my DVD page?" said Joe.

I started to scroll down to the next page. But first, I stopped at the "Bays Park Shorts" section on the BPITS page. There was another little section titled **"Bays Park Shines the Light."**

Guess Who's Leaving?

Which Bays Park girl has decided to move after problems with not just one boyfriend but two? The girl, who did not wish to be named in this story, says she had always been scheduled to move from Bays Park in the next month, but insiders say that life has become too painful for this young lady. "No wonder she's moving," said one source. "She's been hurt badly." Stay tuned for more info next week.

"There is **no way** Luke would have let that get printed," said **Bec**.

"And Rose must have seen it," said Joe. "Remember, she came in after Luke left!"

"Rose Thornton!" I said.

"What?" asked **Rose**, who had just walked into the classroom. Behind her was Ashley, wearing another shade of purple.

"You," I said. "It was you all along."

Ashley looked confused. **Rose just tossed her hair.** "I don't know what you're talking about, David," she said.

"**You did it**," I said. "YOU were the one writing all that stuff. You changed the headline on the Smashing Smorgan story. You added the gossip about Ms. Stacey and Ashley. And the alien interview! You were at the mall that day."

I remembered how I thought Rose and her friends looked like they were dressed for the Oscars. "You must have found that story that Bec threw away in the food court!" I said.

"You can't prove that," said Rose.

"Actually, it's all on camera," said Joe.

He went over to the tissue box that hid the webcam and ripped it open. "Ta da," he said.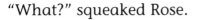

"What?" squeaked Rose.

"I'm sure Ms. Stacey will be very interested in what we've recorded," said Joe.

"That's right," I said.

"Listen, I was just doing my job," said Rose. "BPITS was my page. I wanted it to be **the best page** on the newsletter. Everyone knows I should have been editor of the newsletter, not Luke Firth."

"So you made stuff up?" said Ashley.

"I tweaked the truth," said **Rose**. "People don't just want boring news. No one used to read the newsletter before my BPITS page. Now everyone can't wait to read it. It's a SUCCESS. And you can thank me for that."

Someone coughed in the doorway. We turned around and saw **Ms. Stacey**. "Well, well, Rose," she said. "I think you and I need to have **a little talk**."

* * *

It was bad enough that Rose Thornton turned out to be the newsletter gossip, but **I felt awful** that I had suspected Ashley.

I wasn't sure how to **apologize**, so I waited until the next day at lunchtime. I asked Ashley to meet me under the oak tree.

"Thanks for coming," I said when she walked up. For once, she wasn't wearing purple. "I have to tell you something," I said.

Then I rambled on and on about how I thought she had been the one sabotaging the newsletter. **Finally, she told me to stop.**

"It's okay, David," she said. "I get it. *Boys are confusing*. My mom already told me that."

"Great," I said. Then I pushed her present into her hands. "Happy late birthday," I said.

I had imagined that she would cry when she unwrapped the present. But instead, she just said, "How cute. Victor bought me a stuffed animal for my birthday too."

"Victor? **Victor Sneddon**?" I asked.

Ashley nodded. "Except **his present was bigger**," she said.

"Well, if it was bigger, it wasn't a kitten," I said. "So he got you the wrong present."

"David, you're so **funny**," said Ashley, giving me a little push.

My heart did its $THUMP$ $THUMP$ thing.

"Anyway," she said, "I don't want a kitten anymore. I want a pony."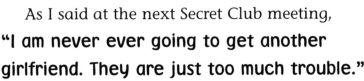

* * *

As I said at the next Secret Club meeting, **"I am never ever going to get another girlfriend. They are just too much trouble."**

Joe nodded. "No girlfriends ever," he agreed.

"You'll **both** have girlfriends," said **Bec**.

"No way," I said.

"Yep," said Bec.

"Not in a million years," I said.

But Bec just kept nodding her head like she knew.

And that's when Joe and I agreed that **girls can be very annoying sometimes.**

About the Author

When Karen Tayleur was growing up, her father told
her many stories about his own childhood. These
stories continued to grow. She says, "I always enjoyed
the retelling, and wanted to create a character who
had the same abilities with 'bending the truth.'" And
David Mortimore Baxter was born! Karen lives in
Australia with her husband, two children, two cats,
and one dog.

About the Illustrator

Brann Garvey lives in Minneapolis, Minnesota with
his wife, Keegan, their dog, Lola, and their very fat
cat, Iggy. Brann graduated from Iowa State University
with a bachelor of fine arts degree. He later attended
the Minneapolis College of Art and Design, where
he studied illustration. In his free time, Brann enjoys
being with his family and friends. He brings his
sketchbook everywhere he goes.

Glossary

abducted (ab-DUKT-id)—taken without permission

ancient (AYN-shunt)—very old

assignment (uh-SINE-muhnt)—a special job given to someone

disappointed (diss-uh-POINT-id)—unhappy with the results of something

discussion (diss-KUHS-shuhn)—a talk about something

editor (ED-uh-tur)—the person in charge of a newspaper or magazine

interview (IN-tur-vyoo)—a meeting in which someone is asked questions

officially (uh-FISH-uhl-ee)—truly or really

privacy (PRYE-vuh-see)—if you have privacy, no one is bothering you

published (PUHB-lishd)—printed in a book, magazine, newspaper, or on a website

sabotage (SAB-uh-tahzh)—an act that purposefully damages property, work, or other activity

suggestion (sug-JEST-shuhn)—an idea or possibility

webcam (WEB-kam)—a camera that broadcasts over the internet

Discussion Questions

1. Why does Rose cause so much trouble in this book?

2. Do you know people your age who have boyfriends and girlfriends? Talk about dating. Do you think you are old enough to date? Why or why not?

3. In this book, David uses a webcam to catch Rose. Do you think that was fair? Why or why not?

Writing Prompts

1. Pretend that you are a writer for your school's newsletter. Write an article about something that happened recently at your school.

2. In this book, David gets his first girlfriend. Have you ever had a boyfriend or a girlfriend? Write about that person. If you haven't had one, write about the kind of person you would like to become your girlfriend or boyfriend.

3. If you worked on David's school newsletter, what part would you want to work on? Would you want to write about sports games, or create the fun and games page, or write about news, or something else? Create a page for a newsletter.

David Mortimore Baxter

David is a great kid, but he has one big problem — he can't
stop talking. These wildly humorous stories, told by David himself,
will show readers just how much trouble a boy and his mouth can
get into, whether he's going on a class trip, trying to find a missing
neighbor, running a detective agency, or getting lost in the wild.
David is amiable, engaging, cool, and smart enough to realize that
growing up is the biggest adventure of all.

Internet Sites

Do you want to know more about subjects related to this book? Or are you interested in learning about other topics? Then check out FactHound, a fun, easy way to find Internet sites.

Our investigative staff has already sniffed out great sites for you!

Here's how to use FactHound:

1. Visit *www.facthound.com*

2. Select your grade level.

3. To learn more about subjects related to this book, type in the book's ISBN number: 9781434211972.

4. Click the **Fetch It** button.

FactHound will fetch the best Internet sites for you!